S0-DZC-279

THE HUMAN PATH ACROSS THE CONTINENTS

PATHWAYS THROUGH AUSTRALIA

Adrianna Morganelli

Author: Adrianna Morganelli

Editorial director: Kathy Middleton

Editors: Rachel Cooke, Janine Deschenes

Design: Jeni Child

Photo research: FFP Consulting; Tammy McGarr

Proofreader: Melissa Boyce

Print and production coordinator: Katherine Berti

Produced for Crabtree Publishing Company by
FFP Consulting Limited

Images
t=Top, b=Bottom, tl=Top Left, tr=Top Right, bl=Bottom Left, br=Bottom Right, c=Center, lc=Left Center, rc=Right Center

Alamy
Deco: p. 4b; Andrew McInnes: p. 8–9t
iStock: p. 16t; p. 17b
Shutterstock
Maurizio De Mattei: title page; amophoto_au: TOC; Photodigitaal.nl: p. 5br; 1000 Words: p. 6lc; Julian Peters Photography: p. 11b; Serge Goujon: p. 15t; Stuart Perry: p. 17t; alexroch: p. 23t; TK Kurikawa: p. 24; JM Smith: p. 26t
National Museum of Australia p. 21tl
Scenic World, Blue Mountains, Australia p. 22b; p. 23lc
BridgeClimb.com Bridge Climb Sydney: p. 21r

All other images from Shutterstock

Maps: Jeni Child

Library and Archives Canada Cataloguing in Publication

Title: Pathways through Australia / Adrianna Morganelli.
Names: Morganelli, Adrianna, 1979- author.
Description: Series statement: The human path across continents | Includes index.
Identifiers: Canadiana (print) 20190112069 | Canadiana (ebook) 20190112077 | ISBN 9780778766346 (hardcover) | ISBN 9780778766476 (softcover) | ISBN 9781427123992 (HTML)
Subjects: LCSH: Human ecology—Australia—Juvenile literature. | LCSH: Australia—Juvenile literature.
Classification: LCC GF801 .M67 2019 | DDC j304.20994—dc23

Library of Congress Cataloging-in-Publication Data

Names: Morganelli, Adrianna, 1979- author.
Title: Pathways through Australia / Adrianna Morganelli.
Description: New York : Crabtree Publishing, 2019. | Series: The human path across the continents | Includes index.
Identifiers: LCCN 2019023324 (print) | LCCN 2019023325 (ebook) | ISBN 9780778766346 (hardcover) | ISBN 9780778766476 (paperback) | ISBN 9781427123992 (ebook)
Subjects: LCSH: Human ecology--Australia--Juvenile literature. | Nature--Effect of human beings on--Australia--Juvenile literature. | Physical geography--Australia--Juvenile literature. | Australia--Environmental conditions--Juvenile literature.
Classification: LCC GF801 .M67 2019 (print) | LCC GF801 (ebook) | DDC 304.20994--dc23
LC record available at https://lccn.loc.gov/2019023324
LC ebook record available at https://lccn.loc.gov/2019023325

Crabtree Publishing Company
www.crabtreebooks.com 1-800-387-7650

Printed in the U.S.A./082019/CG20190712

In Canada: We acknowledge the financial support of the Government of Canada through the Canada Book Fund for our publishing activities.

Published in Canada
Crabtree Publishing
616 Welland Ave.
St. Catharines, Ontario
L2M 5V6

Published in the United States
Crabtree Publishing
PMB 59051
350 Fifth Avenue, 59th Floor
New York, New York 10118

Published in the United Kingdom
Crabtree Publishing
Maritime House
Basin Road North, Hove
BN41 1WR

Published in Australia
Crabtree Publishing
Unit 3–5 Currumbin Court
Capalaba
QLD 4157

CONTENTS

AUSTRALIA

The Human Path Across AUSTRALIA

The Australian flag

Indian Ocean

WESTERN AUSTRALIA

PERTH

The continent of Australia is made up of the country of Australia and part of the island of New Guinea. New Guinea is divided between the continents of Australia and Asia. Australia is part of **Oceania**, a region that includes thousands of islands in the Pacific Ocean. Some people consider Oceania to be part of the continent of Australia. They call the continent Australia and Oceania. Australia has six states and 10 **territories**, including the Northern Territory. It is home to more than 1 million species of plants and animals, and 25 million people.

THE FIRST HUMAN INHABITANTS of the continent were **Indigenous** Australians. They arrived in Australia by boat about 50,000 years ago and still live there today. There are more than 500 traditional **clans** of Indigenous peoples. Each has a distinct culture, and more than 200 different languages are spoken across the clans. Some clans originally traveled from place to place in search of water, and animals for food and clothing. They created a network of routes for trading goods. They moved on foot, and in wooden canoes along the rivers and coast. They also created maps that highlighted sources of food and water. This helped them survive in the harsh desert climate.

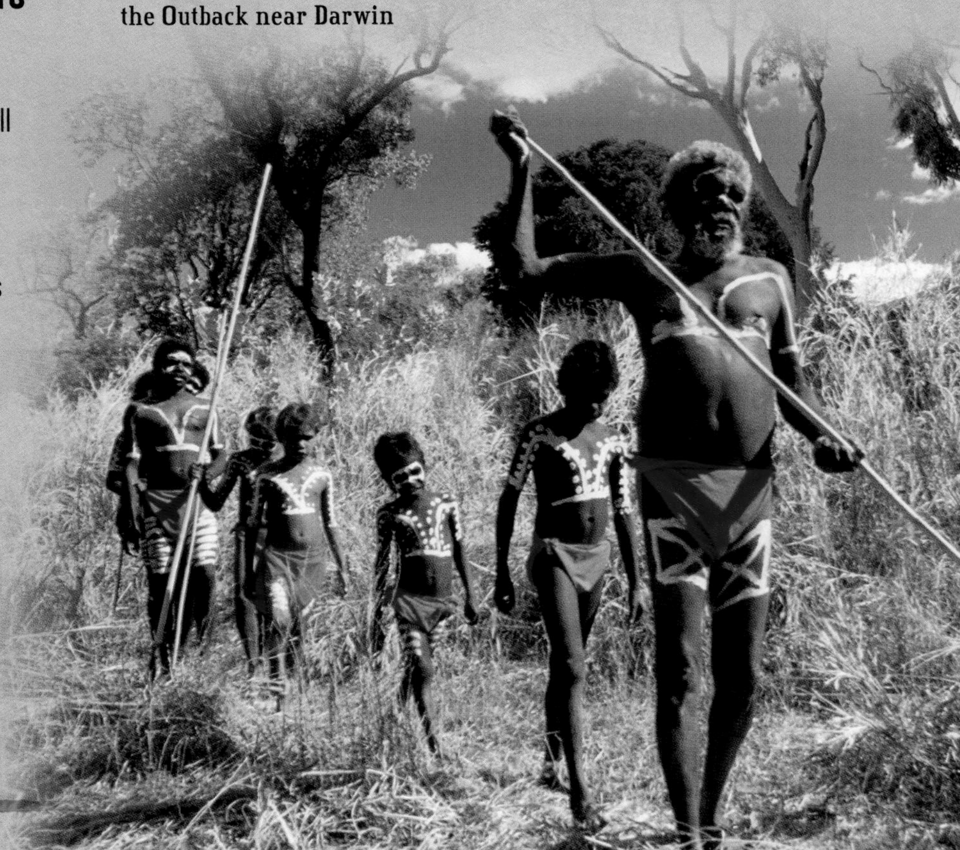

Indigenous people in the Outback near Darwin

PAPUA NEW GUINEA

Pacific Ocean

DARWIN

NORTHERN TERRITORY

QUEENSLAND

BRISBANE

GOLD COAST

SOUTH AUSTRALIA

NEW SOUTH WALES

SYDNEY

CANBERRA

ADELAIDE

VICTORIA

MELBOURNE

TASMANIA

HOBART

Surfers Paradise, Gold Coast

EUROPEAN SETTLEMENT began after British explorer Captain James Cook reached Australia in 1770. Towns grew up on the coast by **river mouths** because of the need for fresh water, and to transport goods by sea. Today, most Australians live within 62 miles (100 km) of the coastlines. Most of the major cities are located near the coast, including the city of Gold Coast. Its suburb of Surfers Paradise (above) is named for its great surfing beaches.

Off-road vehicle in the Outback

AUSTRALIA'S INTERIOR, or **Outback**, is **sparsely** populated due to its huge **remote** desert. Travel is not easy here with few roads, and a tough landscape. People use planes, giant trucks called road trains, railroads, off-road vehicles, and even horses to get around in the Outback. In the cities, people travel in cars and buses, and on streetcars, trains, and bicycles. This book explores the people and geography of Australia, through a variety of different journeys.

A Bus Ride Through PERTH

The busy city of Perth is the capital of Western Australia, the country's sunniest state. To reduce traffic made by individual vehicles, buses are free in the city center. People can take advantage of these zero-fare buses to visit museums, galleries, and parks.

PERTH LIES ON THE SWAN COASTAL PLAIN, between a low **escarpment** called the Darling Scarp and the Indian Ocean, where the Swan River flows into the sea. The landscape there is flat. This means that Perth has had room to grow over time. It now stretches about 78 miles (125 km) along the coast. Today it is Australia's fourth-largest city, with more than 2 million people.

City bus, Perth

Central Business District
Kings Park
Swan River
Heirisson Island
Bus route
---- Free transit area

Modern Perth developed in the late 1800s, when gold was discovered in Western Australia. Thousands of Europeans immigrated there, and by 1900, multistory buildings lined the streets. New suburbs began to develop. Today, the mining industry has helped make Perth a wealthy city. It **exports** coal and **metal ores** to Asia.

Perth, Central Business District

KINGS PARK, one of the largest city parks in the world, is a frequent stop for buses. Overlooking Perth's Central Business District, the park is made up of more than 990 acres (400 hectares) of land. The Western Australian Botanic Garden is located there, and more than 3,000 native plant species are cultivated. Many of the plants are **endangered**. They have been relocated to the park, or grown from seeds collected in the wild. One of the most famous plants in Kings Park is a 750-year-old giant boab tree, which was shipped more than 1,989 miles (3,200 km) from the Kimberley region in northern Australia to be replanted here in 2008.

The famous boab tree, named Gija Jumulu, in Kings Park

Kangaroos on Heirisson Island

WESTERN GRAY KANGAROOS live close to the city on Heirisson Island. This is located in the middle of the Swan River. Originally, the area was made up of many small islands surrounded by mudflats. After years of **dredging**, one single island was created. It is now a nature reserve, where people can enjoy walking and spotting the wildlife that lives there.

Pause for REFLECTION

- Why is the work of the Western Australian Botanic Garden important?
- How do you think plant species become extinct?
- How do you think Perth's parks and nature reserves contribute to people's lives in the city?

Through the OUTBACK on Horseback

Australia is the driest continent on Earth. Much of its interior is a near-desert bush region referred to as the Outback. The population there is small—less than 1 million out of 25 million Australians. Its dry conditions have left it virtually untouched by humans, making it one of the largest intact natural areas on Earth. Settlers first brought horses from Europe to the Outback because they could endure its extreme climate as they transported people and goods. Horses could also work on farms herding cattle and sheep.

TODAY, MOST OF AUSTRALIA'S HORSES are stock horses, a breed used for herding **livestock**. They are now often ridden for pleasure to explore the Outback. The Harry Redford Cattle Drive combines both horseback activities. Drovers, or people who move animals over long distances, take tourists with them along a 150-mile (241 km) route through the Queensland Outback. Aramac, the start of the Redford trail, is a typical small town in the Outback with just 300 residents. The journey lasts up to three weeks, and they move more than 600 cattle along the trail.

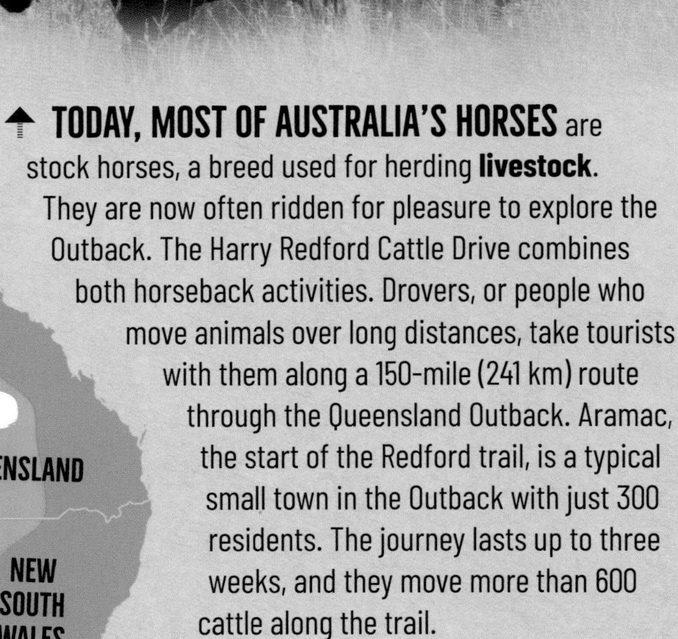

Harry Redford inspired the trail. He was a drover who is famous for stealing 1,000 cattle from Bowen Downs, near Aramac, and moving them to South Australia in the late 1800s.

Cattle drive in Queensland

An early settler home

MOST OUTBACK SETTLEMENTS developed because of either the grazing of animals, or mining for such materials as gold, iron, copper, lead, and uranium. The settlers built simple houses, using cheap, easily transported materials such as **corrugated** iron. Today, early settler homes have mostly been pulled down in favor of sturdier, more permanent homes. Horses have been replaced too. Instead, people use strong, four-wheel-drive vehicles on the rough roads between remote settlements. Light aircraft are also popular, and essential for medical emergencies.

Brumbies in the Outback

BRUMBIES ARE FERAL, or wild, horses that have escaped or been abandoned when farms closed over the years. They have learned to survive on their own and live in herds, ranging freely through parts of the Outback. Australia has more feral horses than any other country in the world! Feral animals damage the Outback's fragile land by eroding the soil. Soil erosion makes it difficult for plants to grow. Methods to keep the animals under control include fencing in fields and reducing numbers by **culling**.

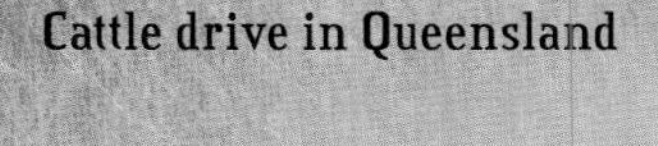

PEOPLE ALONG THE WAY

Jason is a cattle drover who works on a huge ranch in the Queensland Outback. He spends a lot of the day on horseback, moving large herds of cattle from one grazing area to another. The hot weather there can be difficult for him, as temperatures can reach more than 100°F (38°C). But he loves working in the outdoors. He adapts by wearing a wide hat that shades him from the Sun, and makes sure to stay hydrated.

Walk Around ULURU

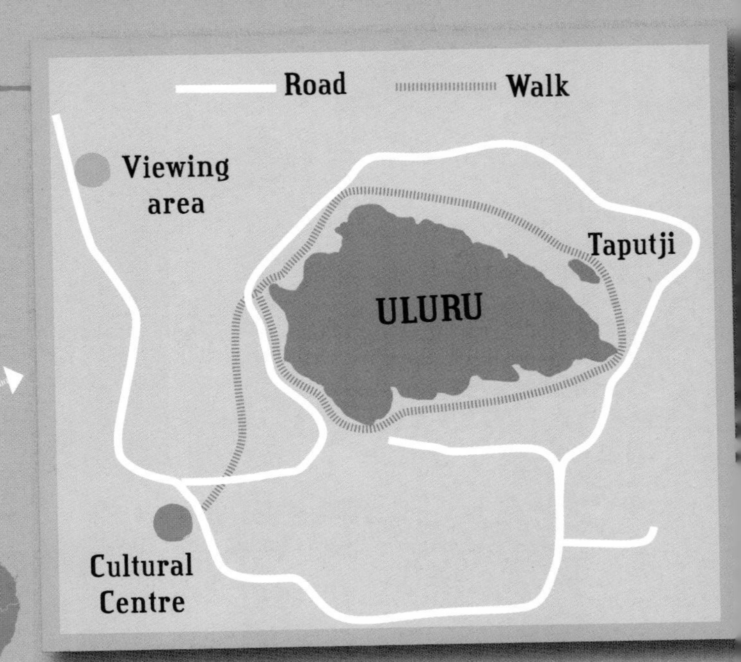

The hot, colorful heart of the Outback is often called the Red Centre. There the land is true desert. Amid the desert is the Uluru-Kata Tjuta National Park. Its water holes, springs, landmarks, and ancient rock paintings make it a magnificent place to explore on foot. Each year, thousands of tourists visit the park. It has been home to the Anangu Indigenous peoples for more than 10,000 years.

ULURU is the most famous feature of the park. It is a massive single-rock formation, or **monolith**, made of **sandstone**. Also known as Ayers Rock, Uluru is 1.5 miles (2.4 km) across, and rises 1,142 feet (348 m) above the ground. Uluru is famous throughout the world.

Uluru is just the tip of a huge piece of rock that extends beneath the ground for several miles. Geologists believe that over the last 300 million years, wind and rainwater **eroded** the softer rocks to expose the formation seen today.

The Anangu believe that Uluru was formed by **ancestral spirits**. The rock is sacred for them because they believe spirits still reside there. Climbing the rock is banned out of respect for their beliefs. It is also dangerous, as more than 30 people have died while climbing it. People now walk around the bottom of the rock, which is 5.8 miles (9.3 km) around.

Uluru (or Ayers Rock)

Emus in the bush

EMUS are one of more than 150 bird species you might see as you walk around the park, along with hundreds of plant species, 21 mammal species, and 72 reptile species. Many of these are rare, and some of them are endangered. Certain species originally found in the area have disappeared due to erosion and **predators**. There are plans to reintroduce some animals to the area, including the malleefowl, common brushtail possum, and the black-flanked rock-wallaby.

The Anangu still hunt in the area, but avoid endangered species. They share some of their traditional bush foods, including kangaroo, emu, and crocodile, with visitors at a four-day festival called Tjungu. During the festival, people enjoy Anangu music and learn about their culture.

KATA TJUTA is a group of 36 rock domes that lies west of Uluru. This is another great place to walk in the park. Geologists believe that the Kata Tjuta was once a single monolith, bigger than Uluru. Over time, rainwater and extreme temperature changes from day to night caused it to erode into separate pieces. During the day, temperatures are around 104°F (40°C), but at night they drop to below freezing.

Kata Tjuta rock domes

- Why do you think it is important for people to respect the ban on climbing Uluru?
- How has erosion changed the environment in the Uluru-Kata Tjuta National Park? How has this erosion affected the animal life there?

Bushwalking in KAKADU National Park

Next we take a **bushwalk** in Kakadu National Park, a remote, protected landscape in the Northern Territory. Its tropical forest and **monsoon** climate are a complete contrast to the Outback. Very few people live in the park—around 500 Indigenous Australians. The walk starts at the little town of Jabiru, on the edge of the park. The town was originally built to support local mines. It is now a base for tourists.

THE MAGUK GORGE is one of many different landforms to visit (and swim in) as you walk through the park. There are also lowlands, hills, and muddy tidal flats near the coast. Outliers, or observation points, give great views. You walk along marked trails, before jumping in a car to visit Jim Jim Falls. This waterfall plunges over the Arnhem Land escarpment. Geologists believe that 140 million years ago, the area was under a sea, and that the escarpment was once a sea cliff that had formed the shoreline.

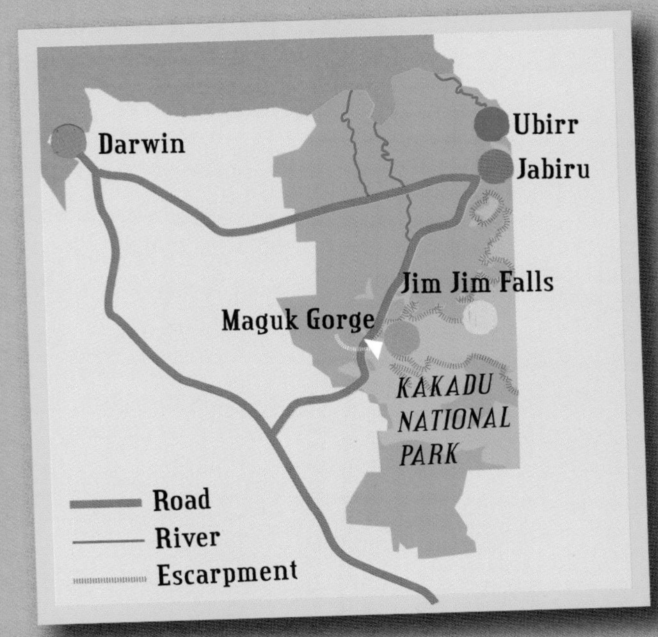

The Maguk Gorge

Rock art at Ubirr

ROCK ART in the park was made by clans of Indigenous peoples—called Bininj in the north of the park and Mungguy in the south. There are more than 5,000 painted rock sites, which are extremely important to the clans. The art often depicts past events such as hunting scenes. Other paintings were made to teach stories about the Creation Ancestors, who they believe created the world. One of Australia's most famous rock art sites is Ubirr, in the northeast of the park.

A saltwater crocodile

SALTWATER CROCODILES are found in Kakadu. At 20 feet (6 m) long, they are the largest reptiles on Earth, and the animal with the strongest bite! Bushwalkers need to be very careful around these dangerous creatures, as people have been killed and injured by crocodiles in the past. Walkers are warned to stay alert near rivers and water holes.

As bushwalkers make their way through the mangroves and banyan fig trees, they are met by millions of birds that either migrate there, or live in the park all year round. The wetlands of Kakadu draw 120,000 visitors a year to see these birds.

Pause for REFLECTION

- How can rock art help us to compare life in the past with life today?
- What can bushwalkers do to ensure they are protecting the environment?

Road Train Across the BARKLY TABLELAND

Let's follow a road train—a huge trucking vehicle used in Australia—to transport livestock raised on the Barkly Tableland. The tableland refers to the rolling plains of grasslands that stretch from the eastern part of the Northern Territory into western Queensland.

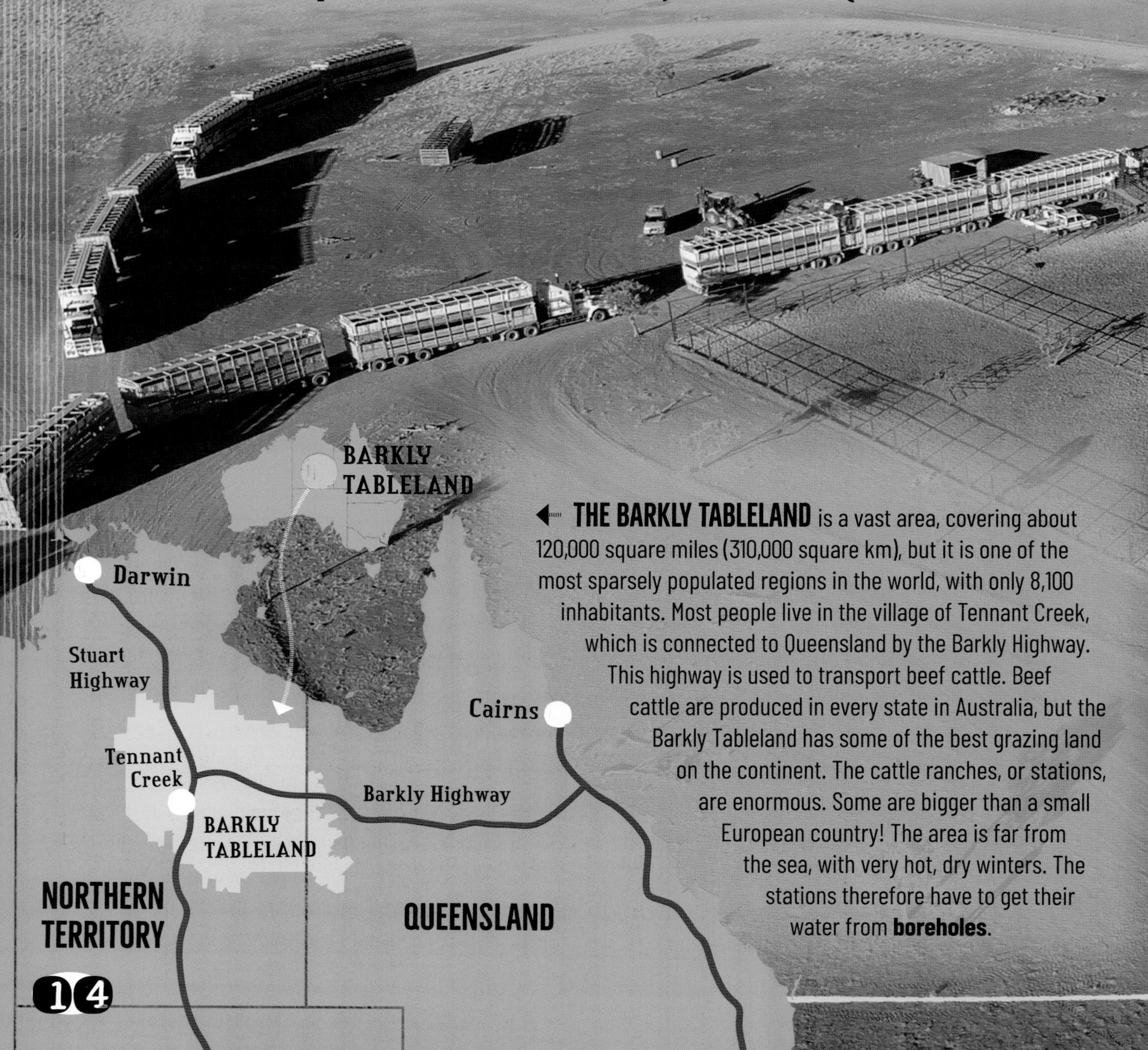

THE BARKLY TABLELAND is a vast area, covering about 120,000 square miles (310,000 square km), but it is one of the most sparsely populated regions in the world, with only 8,100 inhabitants. Most people live in the village of Tennant Creek, which is connected to Queensland by the Barkly Highway. This highway is used to transport beef cattle. Beef cattle are produced in every state in Australia, but the Barkly Tableland has some of the best grazing land on the continent. The cattle ranches, or stations, are enormous. Some are bigger than a small European country! The area is far from the sea, with very hot, dry winters. The stations therefore have to get their water from **boreholes**.

A road train

Beef cattle in the Outback

Cattle ranch on the Barkly Tableland

AUSTRALIA'S ROAD TRAINS pull two or more trailers, and are used to transport freight such as mineral ores, fuel, and livestock. The road trains are so long that they are only allowed to use approved routes. These are straight, empty roads in the Outback which link to major ports. Ports are cities where ships are loaded and unloaded. The road trains load animals at cattle stations on the Barkly Tableland. Some turn north on the Stuart Highway to head to the port of Darwin. Other road trains drive along the Barkly Highway toward the coast of Queensland.

MEAT EXPORTS are important for Australia. It is one of the world's top beef exporters. Sheep are also raised for their meat and milk. Like many countries, Australia sends live cattle and sheep by road to ports, and then by ship to Asia and the Middle East. Animal welfare groups are opposed to the trading of live animals because the journeys are often long and dangerous, and many animals starve and suffer from illnesses and injuries.

Pause for REFLECTION

- Why are some people opposed to the export of live animals? How might the traveling conditions of animals be improved?
- Why are highways important for Australia's **economy**?

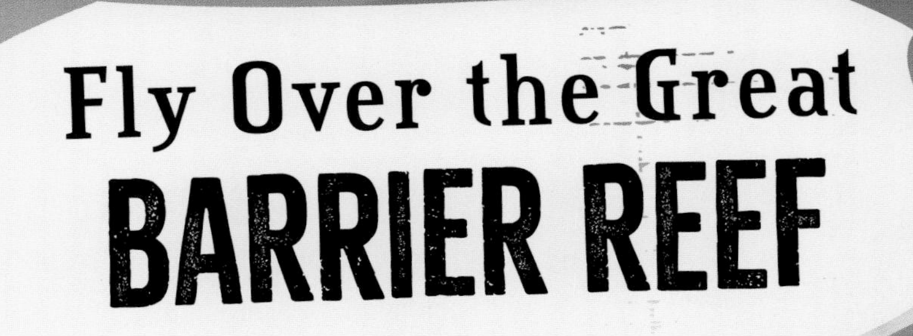

Fly Over the Great BARRIER REEF

Great Barrier Reef from the air

One of the most popular Australian destinations to visit in a seaplane is the Great Barrier Reef, the world's largest **coral** reef system. An amazing 1,430 miles (2,300 km) long, the reef is located in the Coral Sea, off the coast of Queensland. People fly from Cairns to view the main reefs and islands nearby, as well as the rain forests along the coast.

↑ **A CORAL** is a hard substance formed from the bones of tiny sea animals. The corals cluster together to build a large structure called a reef. Reefs are found in shallow, coastal waters because they need warm salt water with a lot of sunlight to grow. The Great Barrier Reef is not one continuous piece, but is made up of more than 2,900 individual reefs, 900 islands, and about 300 coral **cays**.

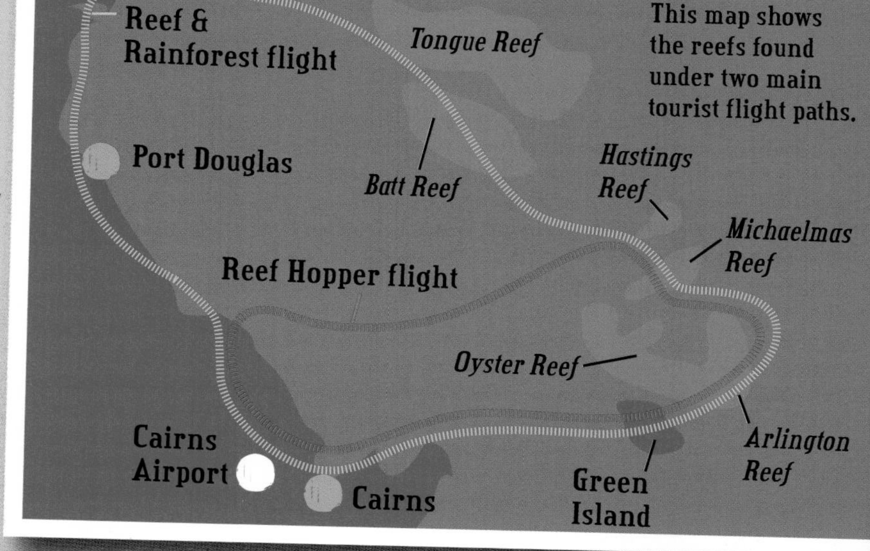

Seaplane off the Queensland coast

SEAPLANES can take off from and land on water. In Australia in the 1930s, they were used to deliver mail and to fly people to the nearby Cook Islands. During World War II, they were put into military service. Today, seaplanes are mainly used for tourism.

Tourism is a very important industry along the north coast of Queensland, creating many jobs. People arrive here from all over the world to visit the Great Barrier Reef. Many will pass through Cairns, which is the only big city in the region.

YOUR SEAPLANE LANDS near a small island and it is time to dive in! More than 1,600 fish species, 5,000 species of **mollusks**, and 30 species of whales and dolphins live in the Great Barrier Reef. Sea turtles are one of the many endangered species you will see on the reef. Despite being protected, the reef has lost more than half of its coral since 1985. One of the biggest threats is **climate change**. Rising water temperatures cause coral bleaching, which is when corals shed their colorful algae, leaving them defenseless against diseases. Pollution caused by humans is also responsible for the reef's damage, from oil spills to farming chemicals flowing into the sea.

Pause for REFLECTION

- What would happen if the Great Barrier Reef disappeared because of the damage from climate change and human activity?
- In what ways can tourism benefit the Great Barrier Reef?

A sea turtle

Export Coal by SHIP

At Newcastle, in northern New South Wales, we board a cargo ship exporting coal to China. Newcastle is the biggest port in the world for shipping out coal, with more than 3,000 ships a year setting off into the Pacific Ocean.

NEWCASTLE was founded in 1804. It was originally named Coal River because of the plentiful coal found in the area. Due to its large port at the mouth of the Hunter River, Newcastle has grown to be Australia's eighth-largest city, with more than 300,000 people.

Australia is the world's top exporter of coal. The majority of this **fossil fuel** is exported to China, Japan, Korea, and India. The journey to China will take between three and four weeks. About 175 million tons (160 million metric tons) of coal leave from Newcastle alone every year. Other port cities, such as Brisbane, also export coal.

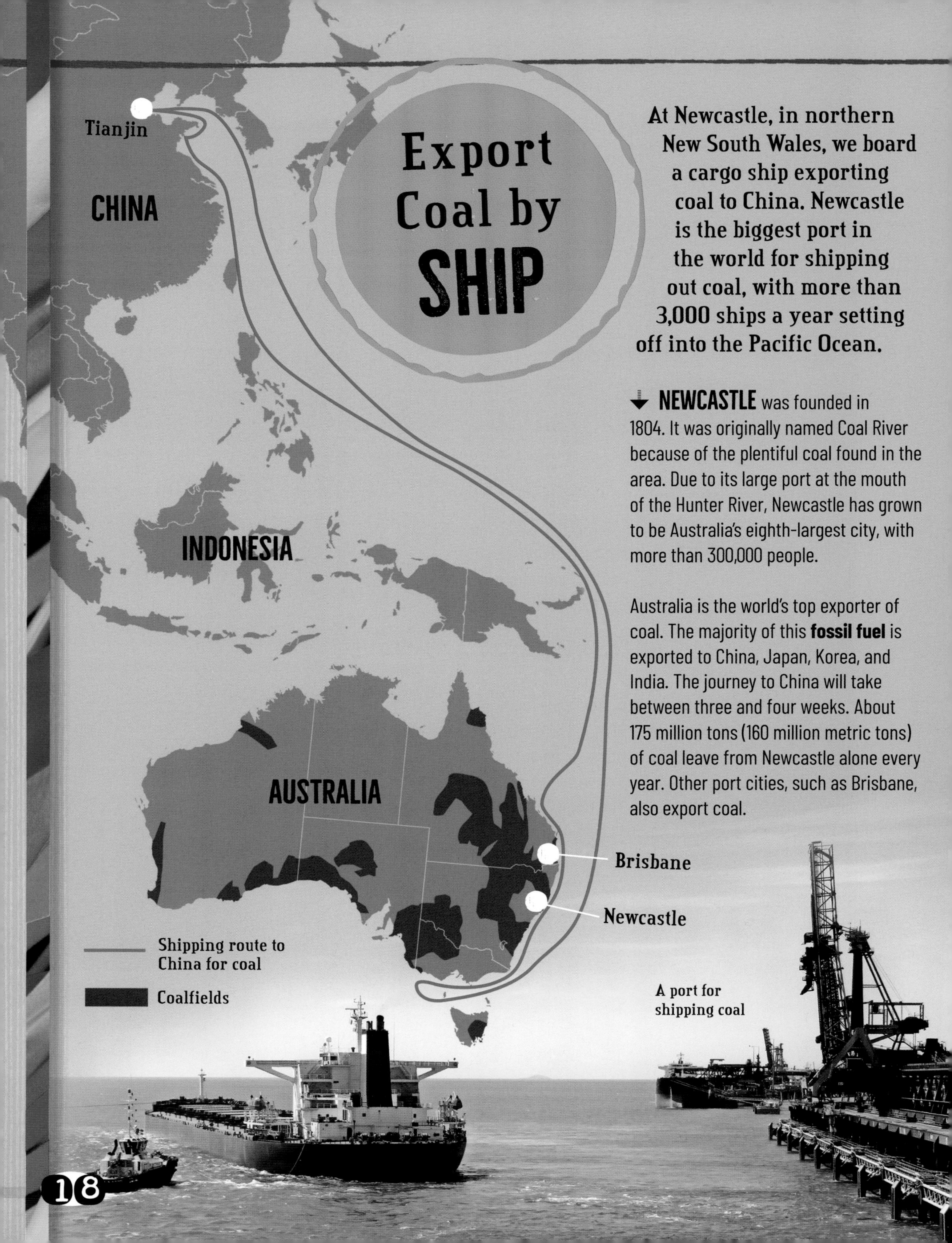

A port for shipping coal

COAL is one of the main fuels used to generate electricity around the world. Most of the coal exported through the ports of Newcastle and Brisbane is taken out of the ground by **open-pit mining**. Transporting coal by ship and burning it as fuel has a very negative impact on the environment. It causes air pollution, and contributes to climate change by warming Earth's atmosphere.

Despite this, mining is one of the most important industries in Australia, and helps to boost the continent's economy—earning as much as $40 billion each year.

Open-pit coal mining

PEOPLE IMMIGRATE from all over the world to Australia to work in the mining industry each year. Some skilled mining workers, such as geologists and electricians, immigrate to Australia permanently. Others live there only to work on a specific mining project. The majority of Australians are immigrants or their descendants. Although originally most came from Europe, today many people come from Asia too. Many Australians try to respect these different cultures. For example, they hold festivals to celebrate many cultures. They also recognize the importance of the nation's Indigenous heritage. In the past, European settlers took Indigenous peoples' land, and thousands of Indigenous Australians died of diseases or in violent conflicts with settlers.

Pause for REFLECTION

- Burning coal has harmful effects on the environment and contributes to global warming. What cleaner alternatives are there to using coal?
- How does the historical treatment of Indigenous Australians compare to the treatment of Indigenous peoples in North America?

Skilled workers at a coal mine

Across SYDNEY HARBOUR Bridge

North Shore
Sydney Harbour Bridge
Port Jackson
Tunnel
Sydney center

SYDNEY

Sydney, the capital of New South Wales, is Australia's biggest city. It has spread out from the original harbor on the bay of Port Jackson. Every day, hundreds of thousands of commuters travel, some on foot, from the North Shore across the Sydney Harbour Bridge to work in the center of Sydney.

BEFORE IT WAS COMPLETED in 1932, the only way you could reach the northern residential areas from the city center was by ferry, or by driving over several small bridges. Journeys around the city were slow. The Sydney Harbour Bridge helped make travel much quicker and easier. Many people moved to the north to escape the crowded living conditions of the busy city center. The bridge, along with the expansion of the road and rail networks, has helped Sydney and its suburbs to grow into a large city. Today, it has a population of more than 5 million people.

Building the Sydney Harbour Bridge, 1930

BRIDGE CLIMBING became famous because, for many years, people risked their lives by doing it illegally. A man named Philippe Petit even walked a wire above it in 1973. Today, people can climb to the top of the bridge legally. Those who dare this feat are equipped with protective clothing and are secured to the bridge by a wire lifeline. The climb and descent take about three hours. The normal walk across the bridge takes about 15 to 30 minutes, depending on how often you stop to admire the views of the city and the harbor.

THE SYDNEY HARBOUR BRIDGE is nicknamed "the Coathanger" for its steel, arched design. It took eight years, and more than 58,000 tons (53,000 metric tons) of steel to build. It spans 1,650 feet (503 m) and reaches 440 feet (134 m) above the water. The bridge provides an essential transportation link between areas of Sydney. With an eight-lane highway, train tracks, a bicycle lane, and a footpath, there are many ways to cross the bridge. So many travelers cross the bridge each day that a road tunnel beneath the harbor was opened in 1992 to ease the traffic congestion.

Climbing the Sydney Harbour Bridge

City center of Sydney

PEOPLE ALONG THE WAY

Angela works as an accountant in a tall office tower in the city center of Sydney. Every day she cycles to her work from her home on the North Shore of Sydney. She uses the special bicycle lane on top of the Sydney Harbour Bridge to keep her safe from other car traffic. More than 2,000 bike trips a day are made along this route.

Around the BLUE MOUNTAINS

NEW SOUTH WALES

BLUE MOUNTAINS

From Sydney, people often make short trips into the country, boarding a train to travel about 62 miles (100 km) west to Katoomba in the Blue Mountains. The range takes its name from the forests of eucalyptus trees. When eucalyptus oil combines with water vapor in the air, a blue haze is created over the land, if seen from a distance.

THE THREE SISTERS are a group of towering rocks, eroded by wind and rain from the soft sandstone escarpment above Katoomba. The Indigenous Gundungurra people who inhabit the area believe that the rocks were once three beautiful sisters named Meehni, Wimlah, and Gunnedoo, who were turned to stone pillars by a powerful **elder**. You can look out at the rocks from the edge of Katoomba, but riding in a cable car called the Scenic Skyway will give you an even better view.

Scenic Skyway cable car with the Three Sisters rocks (left)

THE KATOOMBA SCENIC RAILWAY

is the world's steepest railroad. You can travel on this famous route to descend more than 1,312 feet (400 m) through a tunnel carved into the sandstone cliffs. In the late 1800s, this railroad was constructed to transport coal and oil shale from the mines in the Jamison Valley up to the escarpment. The town of Katoomba grew up alongside the mines, although mining stopped long ago. Now, its main source of employment is tourism.

The Jenolan Caves

Katoomba scenic railway

THE JENOLAN CAVES,

just west of the Blue Mountains, are the oldest discovered open caves in the world. You can take a bus from Katoomba railway station to get there. The caves were once underwater, and contain many marine fossils and incredible **calcite** formations. The network of caves follows the underground section of the Jenolan River, and is made up of more than 25 miles (40 km) of multilevel passages and about 300 entrances. The caves formed slowly over time as rainwater seeped into the fractures in the limestone, which is easily dissolved in **acidic** water.

Stuart is one of about 300 Indigenous Australians who live in the small town of Katoomba, which has a population of around 8,000. He works as a tour guide, showing visitors around the area. He is proud of his heritage and enjoys explaining to the tourists the traditions of the Gundungurra people. They are the traditional caretakers and occupiers of the land.

Drive Along the Great OCEAN ROAD

Driving along the twisting Great Ocean Road, in the state of Victoria, is a great way to discover some of Australia's spectacular southern coast. The road runs for 151 miles (243 km) between Torquay and Allansford. Many people start the trip in Melbourne.

VICTORIA

GREAT OCEAN ROAD

Melbourne

Port Phillip Bay

Torquay

Allansford

Port Campbell

Lorne

12 Apostles

Apollo Bay

Great Ocean Road

Connecting route

State Library Victoria, Melbourne

MELBOURNE is the capital of Victoria. Melbourne is ranked the second most liveable city in the world by the Global Liveability Index. It rates cities on such things as health care, education, culture, and the environment. Melbourne has a population of more than 5 million people. Like many of Australia's cities, it offers a great mix of cultural and outdoor activities. It is where **Australian Rules football** was born, and it is the host of large sporting events. It is also known for its art galleries and libraries.

THE GREAT OCEAN ROAD runs along the Southern Ocean, passing through many small settlements, including the fishing villages of Apollo Bay and Anglesea. These places now welcome tourists who visit the area to enjoy the beautiful landscapes. The beaches are popular with surfers.

Tourists at the 12 Apostles

About 3,000 returned soldiers from World War I (1914–1918) built the Great Ocean Road between 1919 and 1932. It was dedicated to their fallen comrades, and is, in effect, a huge war memorial. Built by hand, it was difficult to construct the road along the steep coastal mountains, and many soldiers were killed during the work. Building the road opened up the coastline for tourism. Today, the Great Ocean Road brings in 600 million Australian dollars a year from tourists who visit the area. It also provides work for over 9,000 people, including jobs in hotels and restaurants.

THE 12 APOSTLES is one of the many important landmarks along the Great Ocean Road. This is a collection of **limestone stacks** off the shore of Port Campbell National Park. The ocean eroded the limestone to form caves in the cliffs. The caves then became arches that collapsed, leaving pillars that are up to 164 feet (50 m) high.

Great Ocean Road, Victoria

PEOPLE ALONG THE WAY

Mick's great-grandfather George helped build the Great Ocean Road. George stayed in the area to become a fisher in the village of Lorne. Mick's family has lived in Lorne for years. Today, there is no longer **commercial** fishing there, but Mick takes tourists out to sea on private trips. He captains the boat while visitors enjoy fishing for tuna and shark.

Bicycle rider in the vineyards

Bike Ride Through the ADELAIDE HILLS

You continue your drive to Adelaide, the capital of South Australia. A popular pastime of the people of Adelaide and its visitors is bike riding on the trails through the Adelaide Hills. This is one of the oldest and largest wine regions in Australia. It is also known for its fruit orchards.

JUST OUTSIDE ADELAIDE, the hills extend about 43 miles (69 km) from the Barossa Valley in the north to Mount Compass in the south. Many biking trails run through the area. German immigrants settled there in the 19th century. They founded the town of Hahndorf and planted the region's first vines. The area's high average **elevation**, over 1,000 feet (305 m), and high rainfall make it one of the best wine regions in Australia. The highest vineyards are at over 1,900 feet (580 m) in **altitude**. Higher altitudes mean cooler temperatures. Grapes grown in cool-climate vineyards ripen slowly, making the wines full of flavor.

SOUTH AUSTRALIA

ADELAIDE HILLS

Cherries growing in the Adelaide Hills

MANY FRUIT ORCHARDS grow throughout the region. In the village of Lenswood, farmers grow apples, pears, and cherries. The fruit is then sold in Australia and overseas. Other major crops include figs and strawberries. The region's varying soil conditions affect the type of fruit grown. For example, cherry trees grow best in lighter, sandy soils, with a good slope on the hillside to help water drain away.

ABOUT 130 GRAPE VARIETIES are grown in the Adelaide Hills. The steep slopes of the hills sometimes make it difficult to use machinery, so growers and winemakers prune the vineyards and pick the grapes by hand.

Australians have developed innovative techniques for winemaking. Special fence posts are constructed to use as much of the sunlight as possible to ripen the grapes. New ways to control pests and diseases are being developed to reduce the use of chemicals. This helps to protect the soil and water in the area, as well as insects and plant life.

Winery in the Barossa Valley

AFTER A PEACEFUL DAY cycling in the hills, it is time to return to the busy, modern city of Adelaide. With more than 1.3 million people, it is the capital of South Australia. Along with Melbourne, it has often been voted one of the best cities to live in the world.

Adelaide seen from the hills

PEOPLE ALONG THE WAY

Kate is a winemaker in the Barossa Valley. Because she is very aware of the need to protect the environment, she has begun to make **organic** wines using fewer chemicals. She often inspects her vines on her bicycle, as it creates less pollution than a car.

Ferry Across the BASS STRAIT

VICTORIA

Melbourne

GIPPSLAND BASIN

Ferry crossing

BASS STRAIT

Devonport

TASMANIA

Hobart

Hop on a ferry to ride across the Bass Strait to the island state of Tasmania. Most ferries leave from Melbourne, and sail to Devonport in Tasmania. Often, the eight-hour journey is overnight and passengers sleep in cabins on board.

BASS STRAIT

A storm in the Bass Strait, nineteenth-century engraving

THE BASS STRAIT is named for British explorer George Bass, who passed through it while **navigating** around Tasmania in the 1790s. About 160 miles (257 km) wide and 310 miles (500 km) long, the strait lies where the Indian Ocean and the Pacific Ocean meet. Its strong currents, hidden rocks, and reefs have caused many shipwrecks. The Bass Strait has been used to transport goods and people since the 1830s, when the British began to settle in Victoria. They shipped cattle, timber, passengers, and mail between the Australian mainland and Tasmania, and to the strait's many islands.

Oil tanker loading in Victoria

THE STATE OF TASMANIA is made up of the main island as well as the 334 smaller islands that surround it. The main island lies 150 miles (241 km) south of mainland Australia. Your ferry takes about eight hours to get there. Scientists believe that Tasmania was once connected to the mainland. About 10,000 years ago, the sea level of the Bass Strait rose, cutting off Tasmania from the mainland. Much of Tasmania is densely forested, with mountains in its center. Most settlements have grown up along the coast, as these places were originally ports where people first arrived. Hobart, the state capital, on Tasmania's southern coast, is home to around 40 percent of the island's population.

Mountain lake in Tasmania

HUGE OIL OR GAS TANKERS may cross the ferry route. In the late 1960s, oil and gas fields were discovered in the eastern part of the Bass Strait in the Gippsland Basin, about 30 to 40 miles (48 to 64 km) off the coast of Victoria. Giant **drilling rigs** are used to take the oil and gas from under the ocean floor. The oil and gas is transported along pipelines under the sea to Victoria. Here, some of it is processed, and some goes on by sea in tanker ships to New South Wales. A new way of producing energy will soon come to the Bass Strait—Australia's first offshore wind farm, made up of 250 giant wind **turbines**.

- How will an offshore wind farm in the Bass Strait change how it is currently used? What might be the positive and negative effects of building it?
- In Australia and the island of Tasmania, most large cities are found on the coast. Why do you think this is the case?

GLOSSARY

acidic Containing acid, a type of chemical that can wear away materials such as rock

altitude The height of a place above sea or ground level, usually given in feet (meters)

ancestral spirit A spirit, or nonphysical part of a person, descended from one's ancestors, which many Indigenous peoples believe guide them

Australian Rules football A sport only played in Australia, with similarities to both soccer and rugby

boreholes Deep, narrow holes made by boring or drilling into the ground, often to find water or oil

bushwalk Named after the low-level "bush" or scrub that covers much of Australia, it is used to describe all sorts of hiking through natural areas

calcite A white or colorless mineral found in some rocks such as limestone, chalk, and marble

cay (coral) A coral reef or sandbar large enough to form a small island

clan A group made up of related families

climate change Change in climate patterns around the world due to global warming, or the gradual increase in Earth's temperature

commercial Describing something done for profit

coral The hard outer covering made by certain tiny sea animals that builds up to form reefs

corrugated Describes a sheet of material that has been shaped into regular grooves to give it strength

culling Reducing the size of an animal herd by killing some of its members

dredging Using machines to remove earth, weeds, and unwanted material from rivers, seas, or harbors

drilling rig A large structure, often found at sea, built to hold the equipment needed for drilling for oil

economy The system by which goods and services are made, sold, bought, and used

elder A leader or senior member of a large family group or clan

elevation The height above sea level

endangered Describes a plant or animal species under threat of extinction (dying out)

eroded Gradually worn away due to natural forces such as wind and water

escarpment A steep, long cliff

export To send goods to be sold in another country

fossil fuels Natural fuels, such as gas, coal, and oil, formed from the fossils of plants and animals

Indigenous Describes people who naturally exist or live in a place rather than arrived from elsewhere

limestone stack A pillar of limestone, a type of layered rock formed mainly of calcite

livestock Animals raised on a farm for profit

metal ores Rocks from which metals, such as iron and copper, are extracted

mollusk One of a large group of animals without a backbone that includes slugs and snails

monolith A single large block of stone

monsoon Seasonal winds that blow at a particular time of year, bringing either very wet or dry weather

navigate To control the direction of a ship, aircraft, or other form of transportation

Oceania The large geographical region that takes in many of the islands of the Pacific Ocean, including Australia and New Zealand

open-pit mining Mining done at surface level

organic Describes a way of farming that uses only natural methods and chemicals

Outback The vast, remote, inland region of Australia

predators Animals that hunt and eat other animals

remote Describes a place far from large settlements

river mouth Where a river reaches the ocean

sandstone A type of rock made over millions of years by layers of sand pressing down on each other

sparsely Spread out thinly in small numbers

territory In Australia, one of the administrative regions that is similar to a state

turbine A machine whereby a revolving wheel is used to generate power

Further INFORMATION

BOOKS

Aloian, Molly. *Cultural Traditions in Australia*. Crabtree Publishing, 2013.

Banting, Erinn. *Australia, The Land*. Crabtree Publishing, 2003.

Rockett, Paul. *Mapping Australia and Oceania, and Antarctica*. Crabtree Publishing, 2017.

Whiting, Jim. *My Teenage Life in Australia*. Mason Crest, 2017.

WEBSITES

www.kids.nationalgeographic.com/explore/countries/australia
This site gives an overview of Australia, from its physical geography to its varied economy.

www.kids-world-travel-guide.com/australia-facts.html
Check out facts and images of Australia, chosen by kids for kids.

www.3dgeography.co.uk/australian-geography
Take a look at Australia through facts, photos, and maps.

INDEX

ABOUT THE AUTHOR

Adrianna Morganelli is an editor and writer who has worked with Crabtree Publishing on countless book titles. She is currently working on a children's novel.